Meet The Gang

Meet The Gang, Volume 1

Mary Tales

Published by Mary Tales Books, 2018.

This is a work of fiction. Similarities to real people, places, or events are entirely coincidental.

MEET THE GANG

First edition. March 10, 2018.

Copyright © 2018 Mary Tales.

ISBN: 979-8230245285

Written by Mary Tales.

Table of Contents

The rain had advanced up the valley like a grey wall. For a short while after they'd crested the ridge, they had been able to look down the trail and see the small stone building they were heading for. But it, and everything beyond it, had soon disappeared under the downpour rushing toward them. When the squall reached them, it was so heavy that it was a struggle moving forward through it.

Zoe had the best waterproof coat she had been able to find. It didn't leak, but the water was hitting her so hard that it forced its way through any gaps and openings. Worse still, she hadn't put waterproof trousers on, and her hiking trousers were drenched in moments. Her socks were soaked as well, and the water was leaching into her boots. The more the weather hit her, the further away the bothy hut seemed.

Her husband wasn't faring any better. His outdoor gear was as good as hers, but suffered from the same problems. "It can't be much further." Derek said, barely audible over the sound of the storm. "They'll be there already, and there'll be a fire on."

"I bloody well hope so." Zoe said. They crested another small rise and, maybe, the darker shape up ahead was the sanctuary they sought. "This was a stupid idea of mine. I'm sorry, we should have picked somewhere more civilised."

"This was a great idea of yours. The weather's just shitty luck. Come on, that looks like it just up there."

The guttering on the bothy had been overwhelmed by the downpour, and a small waterfall cascaded onto the path near the door. After what they had just walked through, this was a minor inconvenience, and they hardly even noticed. Derek pushed the door open and they stepped inside.

The five men already in the small building stopped pulling on their waterproofs and looked at the newcomers. "Excellent timing," said the nearest of them, "we were just about to set off and find you. Come in, but not too far. You're soaking."

Zoe pushed back the hood of her coat, and received one last unpleasant surprise from the rain as water fell off it to run down the back of her neck. She shivered and pulled a face, but composed herself as she turned to face the hut's occupants.

The five men were walking toward them, led by the one who had spoken when they had entered. "You must be Zoe and Derek. I'm Steve. This is Ken, Henry, Mark and Gary." Zoe tried to remember which names matched which face, but worried that she'd need reminding several times before they stuck. They crowded around her and Derek, but mostly her. "You two are soaked, you need to get out of those wet clothes." Steve said, glancing over at Derek and getting a light nod in reply.

"I think Zoe might need some help." Derek said. "Why don't you guys assist her."

Zoe opened her mouth, then realised she didn't know what to say. Wide eyed, she looked at the men who now surrounded her. She was short, and they all towered over her. Derek was above average height, a head taller than her, and all but one of the men around her were taller than he was. She stared up at all the friendly, helpful smiling faces.

This wasn't what they had planned, but it was going in a direction that Zoe liked. She stood still as someone behind her took the weight of her backpack and arms reached in from either side to slide the straps off her shoulders. She had packed far more than was needed for an overnight stay, and when the heavy pack was taken away from her, she felt light on her feet, almost ready to float.

The floating sensation became stronger as Steve stepped forward to open her coat. He had to fold back the flap that covered the zip, then pull it down. Zoe found she was shivering as the only sound in the hut was the clicking as each tooth of the zip opened. The feeling was spoilt a bit as Steve had to work the last bit of the zipper loose two handed. He pushed the coat apart and off her shoulders, and the hands came in from behind and the sides to catch it and take it away.

Zoe's top was wet up the arms from the ends of the sleeves and down the front from the collar, everywhere that water had been able to force its way in. Steve grabbed the hem and started lifting it. She raised her arms so he could pull it over her head and off easily. The top disappeared into the crowd and Steve was pulling her T-shirt from her trousers already.

The T-shirt had clung closely to Zoe's slim frame before it had got wet. Now, it was plastered to her skin from her throat down to the top of her breasts, showing her bra straps and the top of the cups. Water had leached up the material of her trousers and soaked the bottom of the T-shirt as well, but not quite all way up to her chest. Steve bunched the wet hem up all the way to the bottom of Zoe's bra, then paused.

He was teasing Zoe, and all the other men in the room, who watched silently as he started moving it up again. Zoe's arms were still up, waiting for him to pull her T-shirt off. She shivered as the material peeled away from her skin and, briefly, wet her face. Then it was up along her arms and spirited away again.

The hands behind her released the clasp of Zoe's bra. She brought her arms down and held them across her chest before the cups could fall away. Looking around the circle of men who were watching her, she read their lascivious stares and little smiles and liked what she saw. Beyond the men around her Derek was undressing quickly, but pretending not to notice the attention his wife was getting. There had been a script, more or an outline, really, but the downpour had knocked them off that. They were improvising, and doing a good job of it.

Zoe's maid of honour had been the one who gave her and Derek the good word to get onto The Gang. After she and her husband had spent a weekend with them, where cheeky banter and innuendo had escalated into an incredible foursome, she had told them all about a website that would help fulfil all manner of fantasies.

The Gang was a social network of sorts. 'Crowd-source your gang-bang or orgy.' it said on the front page. Everyone on the site was introduced and vouched for by at least one existing member and they were all there for one reason- sex.

Derek and Zoe had many fantasies, and a significant number overlapped. Such as this one. They had hiked a lot in their dating days, when she had been living with her parents after University and he was in a shared house. They had needed to get away from house mates and family if they wanted to get really dirty and loud. There were several valleys in the Lake District and Scotland where they had wandered off the beaten path, got naked and made love in the open air. The urge to do this again had turned into a fantasy where they really went overboard. Zoe wanted to be tended to by a large group of men, and Derek wanted to watch and join in. The Gang had given them the perfect way to get that group of men together.

The bothy- an old shepherd's hut converted into overnight accommodation for hikers- had been suggested by Steve, who had promised that he could make sure they had it to themselves. If the weather had been better, they might have found an open area nearby for the gang bang, but doing it inside the building had always been an option. The way that Zoe was losing her clothes was a neat twist on what they had planned, and it turned her on.

An arm still across her breasts, Zoe pushed one, then the other, strap from her shoulders. She smiled at the crowd waiting on her next move, then slowly dropped her arms to let the bra fall down them and reveal her breasts. They were small, B cups, but they were perfect. Her nipples were long and hard from the cold and the excitement, and they tingled at the attention they got from five pairs of eyes. She held the bra out to her right and somebody, Ken, maybe, took it.

Someone crouched down on Zoe's left side. She thought it was Mark, as she looked down at him, but she couldn't be sure. It was unlikely any of them were going to mind if she got their names wrong after such a quick introduction. He started working to release the sodden laces on her left boot. Ken was by her right foot, working on that boot. It wasn't the sexiest part of her undressing, no matter how turned on she was. Something a bit more was needed, and it was soon provided.

Steve had a lightweight towel. Without moving any closer, he used it to dab water off Zoe's face and then her shoulders. He ran his fingers through her short dark hair, finding the bits that were wet. As he rubbed them with the towel, he gently pulled her head forward and down. This let him get at the back of her neck, but also had her leaning with her hands on his waist for balance. She looked down, and the front of his dark trousers were pushed out, just what she wanted to see.

Henry and Gary also had towels, Zoe discovered, as soft material rubbed at the under side of her breasts, then teased up and around, to be drawn slowly over her nipples. She made a happy sound somewhere deep in her throat. The gentle rubbing continued even after her chest was obviously dry. Steve's exploration with his towel had led him down her spine to the tops of her trousers, then back again.

The laces on Zoe's boots had been released and, at a signal she missed, Steve placed a hand on each shoulder and pushed her upright again. She looked up at his smile, under a determined expression, and knew he was just as turned on as she. Somewhere in the room was her husband. She hoped he could see what was happening to her, it would turn him on incredibly.

Henry had moved around behind Zoe again, and she felt his hands settle on her waist. "Lean back." he said, quietly. When she did as he suggested, she was surprised to find her skin resting against his. She hadn't noticed anyone stripping off. Was he naked, she wondered. When she was balanced against him, his hands came up and cupped her breasts, a finger teasing each nipple.

Gary was naked, Zoe noticed as he crouched before her. Mark lifted her left foot and held it up whilst Gary pulled the boot off it. He put the boot aside and peeled the sodden sock off, dropping it on the floor with a squelch. Mark put Zoe's foot down and stepped back. She couldn't see what he was doing, but when she looked up, she was blessed with the sight of Steve unzipping his trousers, his chest already bare. Realising he had an audience, he hooked fingers in the waistband of his boxers and pushed them down, slowly, with his trousers. A magnificent cock popped out after a moment of teasing. Long and fat, with a big, bulbous head, it was already half hard, and grew as Steve looked at her.

Completely unnoticed by her, Gary had removed Zoe's other boot and socks. Ken had withdrawn, no doubt to disrobe himself. Now naked, Steve stood and watched. Gary was still crouching before Zoe, his hands reaching for the front of her trousers. He released the belt and button, and pulled the zip down. He fought with the wet material for a moment, then pulled them down her legs.

When her trousers were bunched in a wet mess at her ankles, Henry moved his hands to wrap an arm around Zoe's chest and lift her as Gary pulled the material past her feet. While she was off the ground, she felt something nudging between her thighs, and looked down to see the deep red head of Henry's cock poking between them. He put her down and the head disappeared again, but she did feel the head as it brushed against the material of her knickers.

"Why don't you come and stand over by the fire to finish drying off." Steve suggested. Everyone had got naked- the only scrap of clothing left on a body was her knickers- and Zoe had hardly moved past the threshold.

The bothy was a one room building, but the room was broken up into different sectors. By the door there were shelves for storage, stacked with rucksacks and kit. There were steps up from the doorway to the 'bedroom', which had four single beds in it and further storage at the far end. Then there were steps back down again to the communal area. There was a closed solid fuel fire set back into the wall, with the lintel far enough above it that it was possible to put a kettle or frying pan on top of it. Wood inside the fire was glowing yellow as it burned and, up close, it was very warm. Zoe swore she could feel the wet skin of her legs drying as she drew closer to it. In front of the fire a blanket had been laid out and, on either side of it, up against the walls, were large, battered old chairs. Zoe found her husband again, sitting in one of the chairs, his excitement obvious in the erection sprouting from his lap.

Zoe stood on the blanket and grinned at Derek. "You're beautiful." he told her, and she blushed, flushing for the first time since her strip had started. She turned to face the five men they had arranged to meet, who stood in a semi-circle before her. From her left, there was Mark and Gary, Steve was right in front of her, then there was Henry and Ken.

They were all so tall, and quite a few of them were broad, they had the sort of figures built up by cycling, climbing and other regular outdoor exercise. None of them was small, either. Derek was incredibly well hung, and she was blessed to have his huge dick in her life, but none of these guys had anything to be ashamed of. The surprise was Ken. Short and wiry, he had the build of fell runner. His cock, not quite hard yet, was long and fat, getting thicker toward the base.

Surrounded by them, she felt tiny. Short and slim, with narrow hips and the slightest of waists, she had occasionally been called boyish. But there was no way she could be mistaken for anything but a small woman in present company. She should be intimidated, but knew she was in control. They were all rapt with her little body, waiting to see what she wanted them to do.

The fire was warming her back, but there was a different heat altogether radiating out from her crotch.

They were back on the script, so Zoe could direct the action again. Not that she wanted to be issuing orders all the time, part of the fantasy was the loss of control. She'd lay out some ground rules and see where it went from there.

"Now, I know I'm just a tiny woman, but I'm tough. You're all big boys, but if you take a look at my husband, you'll see I'm used to that." They all turned to look at Derek, studying his erection, which was big and fat and proud. He grinned back at them, just a little embarrassed by all the attention. "I want you all to take me, in as many ways and positions and times as you can. Front and back, maybe both at once." The last phrase came out as a husky whisper as she anticipated how that would feel. "Don't be too rough and I'll be up for trying just about anything you can think of. Is that okay with everyone?"

There were nods around the semi-circle. Zoe smiled, trying to hold back the big, dumb grin which would show how she really felt. "Now, I can take you all, but I'm going to need some loosening up and preparation, so start slowly, okay. But first," she dropped down to her knees and beckoned them all closer, "I need you all to come closer so that I can bless each, heh, head before we begin properly."

The semi-circle had closed in, until all five guys were pressed hip to hip, with arms around each others waists, to form a scrum of sorts. Zoe remembered that most of the members of The Gang were bi, and wouldn't have any problems with such same-sex intimacy. The rest were far too comfortable in their own skins to be bothered by it either. She put that thought aside and

concentrated on the deep red heads and thick hard shafts tha
were being presented to her.

Twisting to her left, Zoe turned to Mark. She cupped hi
balls and gently ran her fingers up his shaft, tracing a vein most o
the way to the head. Pulling it toward her, she licked her lips an
then slid them over the hot, smooth surface of his glans. With al
of the bulbous head in her mouth, she swirled her tongue aroun
it and got a pleasing shiver in response.

Releasing Mark, she turned to Gary. His hard on stoo
straight out in front of him, a thick shaft with a smaller head. A
little pre-cum glistened at the tip, Zoe lapped at it with the ver
tip of her tongue and the whole of his cock twitched in response
Taking the head into her mouth, she anointed it the same as sh
had Mark's.

Steve's cock had a very large head, which was a deep shad
of purple and flared out impressively from the thick shaft. Zo
managed to slide her lips over it and lick around the slit, then
when she'd released it, she licked down the under side all the way
to the balls.

In other company, Henry's erection would have bee
impressive. It wasn't small, but all the others in the room wer
larger. He didn't seem the slightest self conscious about it, bu
Zoe decided to give him a bit more attention than the others
He had big balls, which hung low in their wrinkled sack. Zo
cupped them in a hand and gently kissed them before licking u
his length to the head. Her lips engulfed the glans, and kept or
going down the shaft, until she had over half of it in her mouth
She could take it deeper, she knew, but maybe that could wai
until later.

Ken's monster hard on was the big challenge. Everyone was watching, eager to see how she did with it. There was a little pre-cum at the slit, which she spread with her tongue until it was slicked over the big head. She licked around it again, wetting it further, then slid her lips up it. Not quite getting all of the head into her mouth, she pulled back, licked around some more and tried again. On the third go, she got the head into her mouth. Warming to the challenge, she pushed on, taking some more of Ken's big dick into her mouth.

Zoe imagined she heard a pop as she released Ken's glans from her mouth. For a moment, a glistening bridge of saliva joined her mouth to his cock, then she licked her lips and sat back. "I'm all yours boys. Tell me what you want."

The boys were all quiet for a while, pondering what to do next with the sexy woman knelt before them. They could have asked her to go around again, there was no question that she gave good head, but that would have been unimaginative. Steve seemed to be the leader, when Zoe wasn't telling them what to do, so they turned to him. Zoe stifled a laugh as he tapped his lips thoughtfully with his forefinger.

"Lie down and stretch out." Steve said when he had worked out what to do. "We should repay the blessing, I think."

Stretched out on the blanket, Zoe stared up at the giants towering over her. Steve was quietly giving out instructions, as much by pointing as talking. When everyone had nodded understanding, they started moving to assigned positions.

Mark crouched at Zoe's feet, Ken on her left side and Gary on her right, with Henry above her head, his cock waving enticingly over her face. Steve stood back, to direct proceedings. Derek was watching all of this, Zoe wondered how turned on he was. She could look, but she was too fascinated by everything going on around her.

"Take your knickers off." said Steve. Zoe complied, hooking her thumbs under the waistband to push them down, lifting her hips as she revealed the trimmed swatch of her pubic hair. She got her underwear as far as her knees, then Mark took hold of her knickers and lifted her feet so he could remove them. When he lowered Zoe's feet again, he held an ankle in each hand and pushed them apart to spread her legs. For all the heat in the air, her lips tingled as a cool draught flowed over them.

Down on all fours, Mark dipped his mouth to Zoe's crotch. Taking this as a signal, Ken and Gary each took a nipple into their mouths. Surprisingly, instead of offering up his erection, it was Henry's own lips that brushed against Zoe's. A kiss was such a surprise, so intimate, that it took her breath away for a moment, but she soon melted into it.

Mark's tongue lapped up Zoe's slit, teasingly avoiding her clitoris at the top of each slurping journey. It was an incredible sensation, and making her a lot wetter, but not really taking her any closer to orgasm. When she did come, everything being pent up now would come flowing out. Meanwhile, Ken was trying to suck as much as possible of her small left breast into his mouth, whilst Gary teased her right, tweaking the nipple between his teeth.

At a signal Zoe didn't see or hear, the four men pulled back and moved around her clockwise. Ken's mouth dipped down to her pussy. He was going to have to do a lot of licking to get her wet and ready for his massive cock. He didn't disappoint, his tongue pushing deep into her, moving in and out and swirling around like a little prehensile penis itself. Gary's kisses were nibbles and nips just like his play with her nipples, whilst Mark and Henry licked and swirled at her breasts.

Zoe was close to the edge, only a little nudge away from climax, when the licking and kissing stopped again. As the boys all swapped places, she sighed, disappointed, until Mark's lips met hers. She always enjoyed tasting herself from another person's mouth, and Mark's kisses were coated in the tang of her excitement. She squirmed, ready to come, and spread her legs wider, inviting Henry in.

Sensing how close she was to orgasm, the boys had decided to step things up. It wasn't Henry's mouth that pressed against Zoe's opening, but the smooth, round head of his cock. It slid in easily, slipping into her flesh on the juices of her excitement and Mark and Ken's licking. The other three moved aside and let Henry stretch out on top of Zoe as he pushed into her to the hilt. He slid one arm around her waist and she arched her back so he could reach under her.

Lifting Zoe and pressing her hard to his body, Henry rolled over onto his back. When the surprise at the sudden move had passed, Zoe lifted herself, ready to start riding up and down his shaft. His hands on her shoulders pulled her back down to press against his chest, his grin suggesting she had no need to move.

Strong hands grasped Zoe's buttocks, kneading them, pulling them apart, pressing them together. The movements pushed her back and forth on Henry's cock. She liked that, neither of them had to do the work, someone else was sorting out the movements for them. But that wasn't the best of it. The fondling stopped, her cheeks held wide apart, and a tongue traced a wet trail up the cleft to the tight hole of her arse. She clasped Henry's shoulders and let out a long "Ooooh." as her hips started rotating under the probing tongue.

Zoe couldn't see who was rimming her, but they were doing an excellent job of it. The talented tongue ran around the ring of her hole, then jabbed at it, teasing her to relax and let it in. Then it would pull away and there would be kisses against the surprisingly sensitive skin of her cheeks, before the tongue was back at her entrance again.

Strong hands lifted Zoe by the shoulders. When she managed to look up, she saw Steve before her. In truth, she couldn't focus beyond the distinctive fat head of his cock, but that was enough to recognise him by. Reaching down with unsteady arms, she propped herself up and gave a little nod of encouragement. The big purple glans moved closer, nudging at her lips, and she licked at it, wetting it to help it slide in.

The slurping and kissing at her behind stopped, and Zoe guessed what that meant. Her eyes went wide with a little fear, and a lot of anticipation. She looked up at Steve, but, even if her mouth hadn't been filled with his erection, she wouldn't have told anyone to stop. He reached down and braced her shoulders, pulling back so that he popped out of her mouth and just nudged at her lips. He read her expression just right and gave her a smile of encouragement.

The fat head of an erection pressed against Zoe's rear. She tried to relax, to let it in, and was rewarded by the feeling of its tip lodging in her dilating ring. Relax some more, she told herself, breathing out. The cock pushed on, spreading her, moving slowly and easily into her. Still, the feeling when the head passed through the ring of muscle was a surprise. "Fuck, yes." Zoe hissed, feeling victorious. The shaft carried on pushing into her.

She still didn't know whose it was. She didn't care, it just felt incredible.

Once before, Zoe had taken two cocks like this. This time it felt even better, because she was surrounded by men, revelling in the heat and smell of their excitement, which amplified her own erotic ecstasy. Last time, there hadn't been a third erection nudging at her lips, either. She opened wide and took Steve's head into her mouth just as she climaxed.

She shook and shivered, writhing and moving against the three cocks in her. As her excitement subsided, the shaft in her rear was pulled almost all the way out. She wanted to make a disappointed sound, but it pushed back in again, moving her up Henry's hard on and pushing her forward so Steve went further down her throat. The cock pulled out again, back down Henry and moving Steve away from the back of her mouth.

All four of them were moving to the rhythm of the man in Zoe's behind, and he was speeding up. Henry grasped her waist, so that she didn't move too far back or forth, but still she rocked up and down his cock and Steve pistoned in and out of her mouth. With a cry, the man behind her came, pumping semen deep inside her.

There was a lull as they all panted and relaxed a little. Zoe felt the cock in her arse slowly pull out, leaving her open and slicked with all sorts of juices. She expected to feel another head at the entrance, pushing in and taking her on toward her next climax. Instead, Steve pulled back until she could no longer keep her lips around his glans. Looking down at Henry, he asked, "Ready to flip her?"

Henry nodded. He grasped Zoe's waist and Steve held her shoulders, and they lifted her. Henry flopped out of her, and she wanted to complain. Hands came in from either side, and she was turned over so that she looked up at the ceiling. Briefly she registered Mark and Ken at either side of her and Gary sat back with a happy expression, cock slowly subsiding. Now, as she was lowered, Henry's erection nudged at her back passage. The relaxed and lubricated hole opened much more easily for him than the previous cock and, in a moment, he had popped back inside her. They laid her gently on top of Henry, checking with intimate little touches that she was comfortable.

Zoe's legs were stretched out on top of Henry's and they spread with his, leaving her wide open when Mark crouched before her. Henry reached down and split Zoe's lips for Mark to look at the pink passage waiting for him.

Bending over Zoe and Henry, Mark guided his hard on into Zoe, sinking into her to the base. They savoured the sensation for a moment, then both he and Henry started moving.

For a while, they were in time. Henry pulled out as Mark thrust in, rocking Zoe between them. Their rhythm changed, as Henry's thrusts became shorter and faster the closer he got to climax. Every so often, they were each in her to the hilt, and jolts of pleasure, like mini orgasms, pulsed through her. Henry cried as he came, and Zoe felt his juices flowing into her insides.

Mark kept on moving, building up his pace and pushing deep and hard into Zoe. Henry pulled out of her, and she felt the dribble of his and Gary's juices that ran out of her. He held her in place against Mark's movements, squeezing and pinching her nipples with the hand holding her chest. Mark ground his crotch against hers at the end of each thrust and that simple pressure was driving her toward her next big climax.

Ken and Steve were knelt on either side of Zoe, their cocks almost touching in front of her face. They could have been there for ages, and she had been too taken by the feel of the pair of erections in her to notice. To make up for it, she took one in each hand and pulled them toward her mouth. There was no way she could even pretend to get both between her lips at once, so she kissed the head of one then the other, punctuating each change with a gasp of "Yes!" as Mark pushed toward the edge.

Zoe came with a high pitched cry. This second orgasm was even more intense than the first, raising goosebumps all over her skin and setting off fireworks behind her eyes. A moment later, Mark barked out, "Yes!" as he bathed her insides with semen.

"Three down, two to go." Zoe said quietly as Mark pulled out of her. She slid off Henry and managed to roll over and push up onto all fours, swaying a little and savouring the feeling of sticky liquid dripping from her and running down her legs. Ken was already stretching out on the blanket, he knew what she wanted to do next. She could have crawled over to where he lay, but Gary and Steve lifted her up and carried her.

Ken's long, fat cock stood up to greet Zoe. Gary and Steve lowered her carefully onto it. Slick with semen, saliva and excitement, it was easy for even Ken's monster to slide between the engorged lips of Zoe's sex. She took all of him, slowly and steadily, as Gary and Steve let her down carefully. When she was settled on Ken's lap she wasn't sure she could move, but was sure she wouldn't have to.

Steve's hands grasped Zoe's buttocks, parting them. Her arse gaped open for him, wanting him to press that big cock head into her. He was more than happy to oblige. He pushed at her, opened her up slowly, but, despite the liquids lubricating her and the practise of two penetrations already, the big head was as hard to take as the first had been.

Steve pressed against Zoe's rose. She relaxed, and he entered her some more. She breathed out, trying not to think about what she was doing. But that wasn't easy with a huge dick in her pussy and another pressing against her arse. He went deeper, and deeper, and then he was inside her. The fat glans popped past the ring of muscle, and she all but sucked the rest of his length into her. There were stars behind her eyes again. Not quite another orgasm, but spasms of joy and victory.

Zoe needed someone to come in her mouth. She already had semen in her other holes, someone needed to shoot into that one. She looked across at Derek, who was watching everything with a glazed look of lust, cock about ready to burst, and nodded at him to come over to her. Steve and Ken held off on moving until he was ready.

When he was kneeling before her, Zoe looked up at her husband's face. His expression, under the lust, was of adoration, he loved the pure sex that his wife exuded. "I love you so much." she said. "Thank you for arranging this."

Derek bowed down until he could cup Zoe's chin and lift it up to kiss her. "You're worth it. You are so gorgeous when you're getting fucked."

"Let me suck you."

Derek straightened, and his big cock stood out in front of him, the head describing little circles before Zoe's mouth. He moved forward, and her lips wrapped around it, then she swallowed more of its length.

Steve started moving inside Zoe, short, slow thrusts that nonetheless pushed her along Ken and Derek's erections. She lost herself to the sensations as he controlled the speed and depth of all the penetrations. Henry, Mark and Gary were back, fingers teasing and stroking at her skin, cupping her breasts, squeezing her nipples. Derek held her shoulders so that she could just close her eyes and float on the sensations in and around her.

Steve's slow but steady rhythm was breaking down. Every so often, he would make a couple of thrusts faster than the ones either side of them, then struggle to return to his previous tempo. He was getting closer to climax himself. Zoe tensed her muscles, tightening around him and raising a gasp and a series of rapid thrusts.

Nonetheless, it was Ken who came first. He produced a massive amount of come, it felt like, flooding Zoe's insides and splashing out of her. Steve must have felt the action through the thin walls between them as he came almost immediately after.

Zoe felt another big orgasm flooding through her. She tried to channel the excitement of it to the cock in her mouth, and got just the reaction she had hoped for. The head of Derek's cock seemed to grow in her mouth, and Zoe knew he was about to come. It twitched and spurted salty liquid over her tongue. She swallowed some, but more escaped her lips as he pulled out of her.

After a while, Steve pulled out of Zoe, and helped her off Ken's cock- still large even as it shrank. She lay on her back on the blanket, legs spread because she couldn't seem to close them yet, wet with come and sweat. The six men she had just had sat around her, looking down with blissful smiles that matched her own.

"Is it still raining?" Zoe said, dreamily, after a while. Nobody needed to answer, they could hear it drumming on the roof now that they weren't so preoccupied. "I guess it is. Maybe we'll have to stay here a while longer."

"I've told everyone that I'm working on the bothy this week and it's closed to the public." said Steve. "We can stay a little longer."

"Good. When are you boys going to be ready to go again?"

The Layover

"If it's Thursday, I must be in England." Adrianna said, before dropping heavily onto the large couch.

She looked around the room, and decided it was hard to tell which country she was in. She was in an apartment-hotel rather than a hotel room. It was self contained, with its own kitchen integrated with the large open plan living room. With white walls, wooden floors and stylish seating and fittings, it looked like the kind of apartment that would be featured in a lifestyle magazine or be used as the backdrop for an advert. It could be picked up and transplanted in any one of hundreds of cities the world over, and Adrianna had a moment of disorientation.

She was definitely in England, she reminded herself. She had been in China for four days, discussing production and design of her company's goods. Then she had been in Germany for a day, to talk to the people who would manage European distribution. Finally, she had spent the last day in England, talking to the designers. It was exciting running a business with international reach, but, close to a major release, it could be hectic.

Now she was done in England, she could fly back to the States. But she had scheduled a couple of days here to decompress some before the next hectic phase of the product launch. She had booked this short stay apartment and logged on to a website a friend had invited her to join.

The Gang, it was called, a sort of social network. 'Crowd-source your gang-bang or orgy.' it said. Quite a promise, but her friend had been gushing in her praise for it. The men, and the women, on the site were all hot and, when her application had been accepted and approved, she got to see pictures from some of their parties. They really did organise gang-bangs and orgies, and Adrianna knew she wanted to be part of one.

There weren't many members of The Gang in the US. To meet them, Adrianna would have had to travel almost as far as she had on this business trip. So she had planned this layover in England, where there were the most members. After that, it had all come together quickly. And now.... Adrianna checked her watch. Now, she was only a few minutes away from when her adventure was due to start. She just had to wait.

It wasn't long before the door buzzer sounded. Adrianna was unsure what the sound was at first. She was fuzzy, she must have fallen asleep. The buzzer sounded again, and Adrianna hauled herself off the couch quickly to answer it. "Hello?"

"Hi, it's Zoe."

Adrianna's heartbeat sped up. It had started. "Come on up, I'm in 25." She opened the apartment door and stepped outside.

The woman who came up the stairs a minute later was short and slim, with cropped dark hair, wearing jeans and a tight T-shirt and carrying a large shoulder bag. She smiled at Adrianna, and walked briskly across the landing to hug her. "Hey! It's great to see you at last. How are you?"

"I just got in, I'm a little tired."

"We can't have that. Let's go inside, and I'll see what I can do to invigorate you." Zoe put an arm around Adrianna's waist as they headed back into the apartment.

"This is nice." Zoe commented as they walked into the living room.

"Yeah. I've been in hotels for the last few days, and I wanted a break. Plus, y'know...."

"You definitely need a bit more privacy for what we've got planned. Is the bedroom through there?"

Adrianna nodded, and Zoe held out her hand to lead her into the bedroom. She dropped her bag at the foot of the king size bed and turned to Adrianna. "Would you like a bit of a massage, to loosen you up a bit and get you ready?"

"Oh yes, yes. But that might not be so, um, invigorating."

"Oh, I'm sure I can find a way to fix that. We should get undressed." Not standing on ceremony, Zoe pulled the T-shirt over her head and dropped it to the floor. She had lovely small breasts, so petite and firm that she hadn't bothered to wear a bra. The pink nipples tightened up and poked out toward Adrianna as they were revealed.

Adrianna hadn't started to take her clothes off yet, she was too fascinated by the sexy nymph before her, who was now peeling her jeans down her legs. Zoe paused and looked Adrianna up and down. She didn't have to say anything, Adrianna started unbuttoning her blouse. Her fingers fumbled on the buttons, and Zoe was completely naked by the time Adrianna had struggled out of the blouse.

Zoe stepped forwards. "Let me help you." she said, turning Adrianna with a light hand on her elbow and quickly releasing the clasp of her bra. When Adrianna turned back again, she shrugged it off her shoulders and released her breasts. They were bigger than Zoe's, but full and firm, barely sagging when they were set free. Zoe reached up and lifted them, then squeezed them together. Adrianna shivered, she had never had another woman's hands on her before, despite years of wishing for it.

"Can I kiss them?" Zoe's lips were at Adrianna's nipples before she received an answer.

This was all about losing control. Adrianna was going to have sex with a woman and a bunch of men. Completely at their mercy, she was going to give them all pleasure, and get a lot for herself in return. It had been a fantasy for a long time, but until finding the website, and arranging this trip, she had never known how she might make it happen.

Zoe stopped kissing Adrianna's nipples, and they felt cold and tingly as she moved away. "Let's finish undressing you. I want to see you in all your glory." She found the zip for Adrianna's long skirt and released it, letting it drop to the floor. "Gorgeous legs." she commented, dropping to her knees before Adrianna to pull the scanty lace of her knickers down.

Now, all that Adrianna wore were thigh high stockings and the sensible training shoes she had put on straight out of the meeting earlier. Zoe lifted her feet one at a time and removed the shoes. "Let's leave the stockings on, shall we. They're very sexy."

Opposite the foot of the bed was a built in wardrobe, with mirrors panelled into the doors. They stood side by side and studied themselves in the mirrors. Zoe was short and slim, with a slight waist and small breasts. Her pale skin was emphasised standing beside the warm light brown of Adrianna, who was almost a whole head taller. Her breasts were larger, and her waist was much more pronounced, as was the flare of her hips. They had each trimmed their pubic hair- Adrianna's was more aggressive, a thin exclamation point of dark hair, pointing down her mons at her sex, whilst Zoe's was a neat square.

"Lie on your front." Zoe said, pointing at the bed. Adrianna did as she was told. She lay on the bed, waiting, excitement warming the insides of her thighs and the cheeks of her butt.

The anticipation alone was cutting through the tiredness Adrianna had felt earlier. She imagined what Zoe might be doing based on what she could hear. The shoulder bag opened, and Zoe went through the contents. There were clinking and clunking sounds as she searched through its contents, then a low buzz. Zoe put some of the items she found on the bed, but Adrianna didn't look around to see what they were, she would find out soon enough. She spread her legs, so that the other woman might look up and see how excited she was already.

It was a good mattress, it hardly shifted when Zoe climbed onto it. She straddled Adrianna, who shivered at the touch of flesh to flesh, and picked something up from the armoury she had arranged on the bed. There was a spurting sound, then a low squishing. Adrianna guessed that Zoe had put some massage oil on her hands and was warming it. This was confirmed a moment later, when small hands pressed into her back just above her buttocks and slid easily up to her shoulders.

Zoe's fingers were talented. They squeezed tension out of Adrianna's shoulders that she hadn't even known was there, relaxing her and exciting her at the same time. Just like she had said, she was at risk of falling asleep if this carried on. But at least she would have sexy dreams. The soothing hands moved down her back, until they reached her buttocks.

Adrianna's butt cheeks were teased and squeezed, pressed together and pulled apart. Zoe dipped her head to kiss, and then playfully bite, them. She pulled them apart, revealing the pucker of Adrianna's rear entrance. "Do you want the boys in every hole?" she asked, gently.

"Oh yes." Adrianna replied with a sigh.

There was another squirting noise, and Adrianna felt a finger pressing against the ring of her behind. She was so relaxed, and it was so slick with lube or oil, that it slid easily into her, and she pushed her hips up against it. Zoe worked her finger in and out of Adrianna, who rotated against it and savoured all the sensations it offered.

Suddenly, the finger was gone. "Roll over." said Zoe, moving aside.

Adrianna was on her back quickly, looking up at the other woman expectantly. "The boys will be here soon. We should get you ready to welcome them." Zoe said. Adrianna wanted something else first, though. She stretched out her hand until she was touching the inside of the other woman's thighs. Zoe didn't move as the digits slid along the smooth skin toward her crotch. The lips were warm and wet, and Adrianna slid two fingers into her easily. She pushed them in and out a few times, then held them still as Zoe started moving up and down on them, riding her hand.

Reluctantly, Zoe stopped herself, and reached down to pull Adrianna's fingers from herself. "Later. I have to get you really wet."

Adrianna spread her legs and raised her knees, so that Zoe could easily get at her slit. It already pouted open, the lips engorged and wet, but Zoe was on a mission to get them soaking. An expert tongue split the lips, running from bottom to top and stopping to tease her clitoris before heading back down again.

Zoe slurped at Adrianna, saliva and the juices of excitement mixing until Adrianna was wet and ready for anything. She could feel the tingle of an orgasm building inside her, and wanted Zoe's fingers in her to help push her over the edge. But the door buzzer sounded, and Zoe stopped. She straightened, and looked down at Adrianna with a smile, her lips and chin wet with their combined juices. "That'll be the boys. You wait here, okay."

Adrianna nodded. She didn't feel ready to get up again just yet, anyway. Zoe bounced off the bed and walked quickly from the bedroom. She talked into the intercom, then there was no sound for what felt like far too long.

The door to the apartment opened. "Come in, come in." Zoe said. There were footsteps, Adrianna couldn't tell how many men they belonged to, then the door closed again. Did she hear kisses, Adrianna wondered. "Clothes off, boys." Zoe commanded. "Quickly, now. Our guest is in the bedroom and she's aching to meet you all."

Aching was a good word to describe how she felt, Adrianna thought. The warm wetness between her legs was tingling with anticipation, sending shivers through her as the air cooled it. The seed of an orgasm that Zoe had planted in her was waiting for the stimulation that would draw it out of her. It took all of her self control not to reach down and start stroking. But, she reminded herself, she soon wouldn't need to do that. She was about to get multiple lovers to satisfy her needs.

Zoe returned to the bedroom, followed by five naked men. Adrianna had said she wanted at least three, and the Gang had told her they would arrange as many as possible. Now, looking at the array of cocks before her, she had a brief pang of fear- could she take so many. The worry went away faster than it had arisen. She was going to damn well take all five of them, she decided, and then she was going to enjoy Zoe's sexy little body as well.

"Adrianna, these are the boys you ordered." Zoe said. She put her arm around the waist of one of the men. "This is Derek, he's my husband." What a wonderfully English name Derek was, Adrianna thought. And what an incredibly long and thick cock he had. Zoe was a lucky lady.

Turning to the other four men, Zoe introduced them. "Ken, Steve, Barry and Jason. I've had Ken and Steve...." Zoe's voice had a dreamy edge as she remembered an earlier adventure. "And Barry and Jason? Well, just look at them."

Adrianna pushed herself up onto her elbows to look at all five men. They were all wonderfully well hung and, unlike her lovers State side, none of them were circumcised. She didn't know if that was going to make any difference, they were all already so hard that their foreskins had pulled back and tucked up behind the heads of their cocks. She would have to see if they tasted different, or felt different. She licked her lips and smiled at them.

"So, which of the boys do you want?" Zoe asked.

"All of them." Adrianna replied, with a bit of a croak.

"Of course. I phrased the question wrong. Which of the boys do you want first?"

Adrianna couldn't possibly make her mind up. She would have to make the choice as random as possible. Closing her eyes, she held her right arm out, pointing. She moved her arm back and forth, trying to forget where each of the boys was relative to her, stopping randomly. Opening one eye, she found she was pointing at Ken. He smirked and stepped forward. Rubbing his hands together, he asked, "So, how would you like to start?"

Adrianna laid back and opened her legs even wider. "I need a cock in me. Zoe's got me almost there. Fuck me, fuck me, fuck me. Two at once. Three at once if we can. But let's start with you In me. Now."

Ken moved quickly but gracefully onto the bed and planted himself between Adrianna's legs. Holding his erection, he stroked the head up and down between her lips, but didn't push in. "Don't tease her, Ken, that's just mean." Zoe said. Ken found Adrianna's entrance, lodged the tip of his cock there, then put his weight behind it to push easily into her.

Adrianna had a couple of lovers back in the States. Occasionally, she had taken them both at once. Still, neither of them was as big as Ken, or any of the other men standing around the foot of the bed and watching as he took her. It had been too long since she had been properly fucked by a good, big, dick. Ken filled her, stretching her in the lovely way she remembered. She reached up and wrapped her arms around his shoulders and squeezed her thighs tight against him.

"Ready to let the boys take control?" Zoe asked. Adrianna hadn't even noticed her coming up to stand by the head of the bed. Or the two men who had got onto the bed either side of her and Ken. She thought about what Zoe's question meant. Five big cocks, taking her one after the other or, as she remembered demanding, two or three at once. It would be extreme, overpowering. Of course she wanted it. She nodded eagerly.

"You do?"

"Yes. Absolutely."

"You heard her boys. Do what you do so well." Zoe stepped back and sat on one of the chairs from the breakfast bar. Adrianna wondered when that had come through to the bedroom, but only for a moment. Ken's arms wrapped around her shoulders and waist and lifted her up. With the help of the men either side of them, he turned her over, so that she was on top of him. Hooking his ankles over hers, he spread their legs.

Ken's big hands settled on Adrianna's butt cheeks and squeezed them, then pulled them apart. She wondered if he could feel how fast her heart was beating. Two men at once! She'd done it before, a couple of times, but never with such well endowed studs as these. Something pressed against the entrance to her ass, then pushed in. A finger, thicker and longer than Zoe's digit, it pumped inside her a few times, and she bucked back against it.

The finger pulled out of her. Its owner, satisfied that Adrianna was ready for him, presented something completely different to her entrance. The head of the big cock nudged against her. She relaxed, and let it push, press and enter her. As more and more of the awesome erection fed into her and she felt filled like never before, the seed of orgasm Zoe had planted in her blossomed.

"Fuuuuuuck!" Adrianna cried as she came. It exploded out from somewhere between the two cocks in her, filling her and flickering out to fingers, toes and scalp. There were lights behind her eyes, and a floating sensation as the hard ons inside her lifted her up. And this was just the first of what she knew would be many, many orgasms to come. She buried her head in Ken's shoulder and rode the incredible sensations.

The movement of the cock in her butt brought Adrianna back to her senses, slowly. It was just moving a short distance, grinding, it felt like, against the head of the cock in her pussy. She loved the sensations, voicing her pleasure with a groan.

Gentle hands took hold of Adrianna's chin, and lifted her face up and moved it to the right. She was staring straight at the purple head of another big erection, warm and bobbing before her face. She looked up at a flat stomach, broad chest and then the smiling face of Steve. She nodded at him, then opened her mouth wide. Steve moved his hips to put his cock between her lips.

Strong hands grasped her hips, and the cock in Adrianna's ass started pumping harder in and out of her. The movements pushed her along Ken's erection, then he started moving as well, to accentuate the sensations. Steve's hard on pumped in and out of her mouth. All she could do was hold her jaw open and keep her lips wet as they slid up and down the shaft.

There was another orgasm building inside Adrianna, but she was beaten to it by the man in her behind. The hands around her waist grasped tight and pulled her hard against him, holding her there as he pumped deep inside her with a gruff shout. He held her there for a while, then pulled slowly out. As she felt his juices dribbling out of her, she sensed Ken was about to start moving faster and deeper inside her.

Not held back by the weight of another man atop them, Ken was able to move faster, and make longer thrusts, in Adrianna. Muffled by the cock in her mouth, she gave voice to her mounting climax as moans deep in her throat. She had to lift her lips away from Steve's cock as she cried out her second orgasm. Ken pushed up and came inside her almost simultaneously.

Steve didn't allow her any time to come down again. He lifted her off Ken, laid her on the bed and was between her legs in moments. She had hardly even finished milking Ken, the last couple of drops of cum dripped from his juice coated cock as Steve slid easily into her. He hooked his arms under her knees and lifted her legs up until they touched her chest, letting him push even deeper into her.

"Hard?" Steve asked. Adrianna nodded enthusiastically, and soon the heavy slap of Steve's thighs against her butt cheeks at the end of each thrust was making time with her cries of joy. There was so much power behind his movements that he pushed her across the bed until her head hung off the edge. Before she could go any further, another pair of hands pressed against her shoulders to hold her in position.

Adrianna opened her eyes and stared up, to see who the hands belonged to. Her view was filled by another magnificent erection, which bobbed over her head. As he crouched more, the glans tapped against her lips. Tipping her head as far back as possible, she opened her mouth and took it in.

The cock moved in and out of Adrianna's mouth, rubbing along her tongue, as Steve hammered into her. She still didn't know, or care, who she was sucking. If she could, she would take him deeper, open her throat to him. But not while Steve was pumping into her.

As if on cue, Steve's thrusts became shorter and even faster. He came deep inside her, and it felt like she was overflowing with semen. He held his position for a while, before pulling out and gently laying her legs on the bed. Hearing movement, Adrianna held up a hand, signalling the new man approaching her to stop for a moment. Then, with out letting the cock out of her mouth, she signalled her intentions. It might have looked like crazy waving, but it was soon clear that she was understood.

Adrianna hadn't deep throated before, but she had practised with her favourite dildo a few times. With a hand held up, she signalled for the man above her to push his cock deeper into her throat. It pressed against the back of her mouth. She signalled for him to stop, relaxed for a moment, then had him push in some more. The big dick was in her throat, and she tingled with a sense of victory. She waved her hand back and forth, and he started moving in and out, gently fucking her mouth and throat.

She couldn't move her head, and most of her vision was taken up by the shaft and balls moving to and fro, but just, at the edges of her vision, Adrianna was vaguely aware of figures crowded around to watch her. The attention, and the sensations, sent shivers through her. It wasn't quite another orgasm, though. Deep throating the mystery cock was incredibly erotic, and the knowledge that she had such an eager audience made it more so, but it wasn't going to be enough to push her over the edge, even as keyed up as she was. She wanted to come and come and come, so, with a little regret, she signalled for her partner to pull out of her throat.

"I need you in my ass." Adrianna said, with a bit of a croak.

The man who had been fucking her throat leant forward and said, "With pleasure." She had enough time to register that it was Derek, before his strong hands on her shoulders, and another pair holding her ankles, rolled her over with ease. As he climbed onto the bed and moved round behind her, Adrianna looked around. His wife was watching, with a dreamy expression and a dirty smile. She was also working Ken and Barry back to stiffness, pumping their cocks in her little hands and occasionally kissing the purple heads. Derek and Zoe might just be the perfect couple, Adrianna thought, as a big hard on pushed firmly but carefully into her behind.

Almost over the edge, Adrianna threw her head back, closed her eyes and let out little cries of pleasure with each thrust. She grasped the sheets with both hands, and pushed her hips up to press back against Derek's cock. Shaking and shivering,

she felt another climax wash over her. She clenched her muscle
around Derek, holding him in her and drawing an exclamation
of surprise and pleasure. Buried deep inside her, he came, hard.

After a while, Derek pulled out and sat back. Adrianna wa
exquisitely aware of the juices dribbling out of her, and sh
squirmed against the sheets as they did.

Normally so good with numbers, Adrianna had an inkling
that she had to count something. She worked out what sh
should be tallying when fingers stroked her waist and buttocks
"Arse or pussy?" Jason asked quietly.

"Pussy." Adrianna said, drawing the word out as she moved so
that her butt was up in the air whilst her head and shoulders wer
still pressed against the sheets. Grasping her waist and pulling
her to him, Jason thrust straight into her. With all the semen
already in her, he slicked back and forth with ease. She was stil
so excited, and he stretched her and pressed against her clit with
every thrust, that she was soon speeding toward yet another
climax.

Light kisses were landing on Adrianna's forehead, nose and
cheeks, then her lips. She opened her eyes and found that Zoe
was on the floor before the bed, with the other four guys behind
her, watching the action.

Playing for the audience, Jason started drawing out his
strokes, pulling out until only the tip was in Adrianna, then
thrusting hard into her. The pounding had Adrianna on a
permanent plateau of pleasure. Zoe glued her lips to Adrianna's
open mouth and kissed her hard.

Adrianna lost track of how long she was on this orgasm high
until she was aware of yet more semen pumping deep inside her

She floated on the ecstasy for a while, as Jason laid her gently on the bed and stretched out beside her.

Hands lifted Adrianna up and moved her around, until her head was resting on the pillows, with a man sat against the wall either side of it. There were another two men down by her feet. At the foot of the bed was Zoe, crouching between Adrianna's feet and grinning. Ken stood behind her.

"How do you feel?" Zoe asked.

"Incredible." Adrianna stretched her arms out to either side, and when they came down, they each landed on a big, and stiffening, penis. "Just incredible."

"You want to go again?"

"Soon, yes. I want you. I haven't had you yet."

"Let me lick you out. I want to taste all that come from inside you." That turned Adrianna on incredibly, the idea of Zoe licking up the mingled semen of three different men from her pussy. She was going to ask if she could taste it, but the other woman seemed to read her mind, and said, "And if I can borrow Ken while I do it, then you can do the same to me."

Adrianna's legs practically shot open, and Zoe moved up between them. As she leaned forward and laid the flat of her tongue against Adrianna's slit, Ken climbed onto the bed and guided himself into her. Her tongue probed between Adrianna's lips, then was pushed deeper as Ken thrust into her.

Light, talented touches played over Adrianna's skin, from her thighs up to her shoulders. Her breasts, in particular, got a lot of attention. Soon, different lips had each nipple between them teasing them and holding them as tongues flicked at them. She repaid the attention with the steadiest strokes she could manage of the two cocks she held.

Adrianna could hardly concentrate as Zoe's tongue cleaned her out and Steve's and Derek's played with her nipples. She tried to focus on Ken's face, watching the expressions as he thrust in and out of Zoe. At first, his mouth tightened each time he started a thrust, and she used this signal to tell her that Zoe's tongue would be pressed even harder into her again. But as he became more and more excited, his lips split, and he had the hint of a smile. As he and Zoe neared climax, he looked up and caught Adrianna's eyes. They stared at each other as his thrusts became faster and he pulled Zoe to him so he could come deep inside her. She finally lifted her mouth from Adrianna's pussy to cry out her own pleasure.

Again, Zoe's lips and chin were wet and glistening. This time, there was semen mixed in with the saliva and pussy juice. She grinned, and pulled her husband toward her for a kiss. As Derek licked and kissed her face, Ken started to pull out of Zoe. She reached back to cup her pussy as he left it, holding in as much as possible of his juices. "Round two." she said, as Ken and Derek helped her lie back with her head hanging over the edge of the bed. "Are you ready? Do you mind if I join in?"

Adrianna moved slowly and carefully, as if drugged from all the pleasure she had already experienced. She got herself onto all fours between Zoe's legs and stared up the lovely body. "Yes, and no." she said quietly. "The boys all deserve to come at least once more, and I think I'll need your help for that. Why don't you see how much of Barry you can swallow, whilst Derek fucks my cunt."

The other players were in position quickly. Adrianna watched Zoe tilt her head back to take Barry's erection between her lips. As she did this, she lifted the hand that had been shielding her slit, and Adrianna watched a blob of white liquid seep out between the lips. She dipped her head down and teased the tip of her tongue out to taste it.

Derek presented the head of his hard on to Adrianna's pussy. She was tender and sensitive after the pounding she had just received- more than she had thought- but he seemed to sense this and fed himself into her slowly. As he started a slow and gentle rhythm in and out of her, she lapped at his wife, licking another man's semen from her.

The layover was for a day and a half, and Adrianna knew she was going to spend most of it with these six people. She was going to fly home with a warm ache all through her body from giving and receiving pleasure non-stop, and it was going to be worth it.

The only problem was that The Gang had so few members in the States. Perhaps she should start recruiting more.

Or she could just arrange lots more business trips to Britain.

"Working on your birthday?" Beth asked.

"I know. I was hoping being self employed would mean I could take days off when I wanted." Yvonne said, with a sigh. "But, well, Tony wants to run some visuals past me, and he says they'll look best laid out on a big table. Sounds silly to me, but here I am."

"And all dressed up, I see."

"Well, he did promise me a fancy meal afterwards. So I put on a nice sexy dress." And the very skimpy underwear he got me, she didn't add. They could have some fun in the car on the way home from the meal.

"Tony called ahead and booked you meeting room two. There's almost no-one else in the building. They've all decided to go home early. Head on up."

Both the meeting rooms were on the top floor of the building. The other three floors were filled with short term offices, used by other self employed people and small companies that only needed them occasionally. Yvonne and her husband had used the offices regularly and not only improved their productivity, but made several useful connections, both professional and personal. Beth was both, but they tried to keep their conversations professional when they were in the building she owned and managed.

Meeting Room two was large and open, with light wood flooring and a window that dominated the whole of one wall. The main item of furniture was a grand oval meeting table in the

middle of the floor, surrounded by matching chairs. Yvonne pu[t]
her bag on the table, then went to stand by the window.

The window overlooked a small park, beyond which wa[s]
another, more mundane, office building. Yvonne watched th[e]
late afternoon traffic of office workers escaping early with a littl[e]
smile. She and Tony had been like that, once, before leaving t[o]
start their own business. Ironically, they now worked more hour[s]
than they had before, but they wouldn't go back if they coul[d]
help it.

The door opened, and Yvonne turned at the sound. The ma[n]
striding toward her wasn't her husband, but a stringy, tightl[y]
muscled chap wearing shorts and a tight, long sleeved top. H[e]
was opening the large satchel slung over his shoulder. His fac[e]
looked familiar, but Yvonne was more interested in checkin[g]
him out physically. She did like a cyclist's body, all that lea[n]
definition and tight buttocks. He smiled at her and pulled thre[e]
envelopes from his bag.

"I've got a delivery for you." the cycle courier said, handin[g]
over one of the smaller envelopes.

This was unexpected, but not entirely unexpected. Tony di[d]
like to spring surprises to mark birthdays and anniversaries. A[t]
least she was dressed up for whatever he had planned. Consciou[s]
that the courier was watching her with an uncommon interest[,]
Yvonne tore open the envelope and pulled a card out of it.

The writing on the card was in her husband's distinctive[,]
sharp script.

'The courier is in The Gang. Give him your knickers and he'l[l]
tell you how to get them back. T.'

Yvonne looked up sharply at the courier, who was trying t[o]
look disinterested and not smile. Now she remembered where

she had seen him before. She and Tony had received their invitation to the website dedicated to arranging gang bangs and orgies but, she thought, not taken advantage of it yet. Obviously, Tony had used it when she wasn't around so that he could organise a birthday surprise for her.

The courier opened the larger, padded, envelope, ready for Yvonne to fill it. If she did as the card said, he wasn't going to look away. She grasped her dress just below the waist and started bunching up the material, pulling the hem up until she could reach under it and hook her hands into the lace of her underwear. She pulled her panties down her legs and stepped out of them.

Holding out the near-nothing she had just taken off, Yvonne dropped the wisp of material into the offered envelope. The courier closed it and handed over the last one. The tremble of her fingers gave away Yvonne's excitement as she opened it.

'Flash the nice man, or more, if you'd like, then let him leave. Wait in your car for the next instruction. T.'

"I've forgotten your name. I'm really sorry."

"I'm Jason."

"The card says I should do this." Her dress was simple but sexy, light blue, with a low neckline to show off her cleavage to best effect, it buttoned all the way down the front. She reached down and released the bottom three buttons, then pulled the front apart. Jason watched as her shaved mound was revealed, paying particular attention to the neat slit of her pussy lips. In the short time since he had handed her the first card, Yvonne's excitement had started to ramp up, and the lips were already darkening as the blood began to pump to them. "Will you be seeing this again later?" Yvonne asked, trying to keep her tone as even and non-committal as possible.

"I believe so."

"Would you like a taste to be going on with? Something to show you what to look forward to?"

"That's quite alright, I'll wait. The anticipation makes it better later." Jason's smile suggested he had done this sort of thing before, and he knew what he was talking about. He put the large envelope back into his satchel, gave a little nod and walked out of the room.

Yvonne couldn't make her legs move at first. She leant against the table whilst her heart hammered away. It was really happening. She and Tony had talked about their fantasies, turning each other on imagining what they would do when they got up the nerve to bring in The Gang. Hers had been to have a series of dirty encounters, in places where she risked discovery, as she travelled from place to place hunting clues. They had never made clear what the clues were for, that never mattered in the build up to sex. But now she knew- it was all part of a treasure hunt, the prize the return of her expensive, underwear.

Picking her bag up, Yvonne straightened her shoulders and back and walked purposefully to the elevators. She looked more composed than she felt. The elevator doors were highly polished metal, giving her a slightly hazy reflection of herself to consider. She was about average height, but slim, her figure, after two children, as good as ever thanks to the cycling and swimming she had started doing a year before. Her auburn hair fell in thick waves to her shoulders, framing an attractive face with what her husband referred to as blow job lips, full, soft and loaded with character. The men she met on her treasure hunt weren't going to be disappointed. The lift pinged and the door opened, taking away her reflection and opening onto the next part of her adventure.

In the foyer, Yvonne could sense Beth's eyes on her as she walked toward the reception desk. The other woman didn't often work front of house, staying back in her office chasing up new clients. Of course, it had been Beth who had introduced Yvonne and Tony to The Gang. With the smile she was failing to hide, she had to know what was going on. "Away so soon? Did the courier deliver something important?" Beth asked, unable to make the questions sound innocent.

"Well, he took something, actually. I've got to head out and.... meet some people." Yvonne's reply was an equally obvious lie.

"Well," Beth stood and leaned over the desk, holding out a key ring, "if you should need to get back in later, these are master keys. I'm closing the offices a little early today."

Yvonne took the keys, and put them straight into her bag. She was sure there would be a significance to them, but felt that she'd have to wait to find out what it was. "Thanks. Well, erm, I'll see you later."

"Maybe. Have fun, birthday girl."

Yvonne's car was parked under the building next door. The basement car park had spaces reserved for clients of Beth's office space and wasn't open to the public. Yvonne flashed a pass to the man who operated the gates and walked over to her Mini, parked in one of the furthest corners.

Sat in the car, Yvonne realised she hadn't buttoned her dress up again, as the front split open, revealing her pussy. It would be almost impossible for anyone to look through the window and see it, but if she didn't button it up, she would know she was flashing the world as she drove along. She liked that idea, and spread her legs to let her sex tingle in the cool air.

There was a tap on the window beside Yvonne's head. She jumped, and quickly closed her legs. What if the attendant had walked over and seen her flashing. She looked to her right, and was greeted by the sight of a man in jeans standing beside her car. Only the space between his waist and knees was visible, and the bulge in the front of his tight trousers drew her attention. Not the attendant, then.

The fingers that had tapped the window moved in a circle. Yvonne understood the message, and pressed the button to open the window. The man didn't move to look through the window. She would have to speak to his crotch, which wasn't such a bad thing. "Do you have the next clue?" she managed to say, her voice warbling a little with nervousness.

"I do."

"There's a forfeit, isn't there?"

"Every clue requires something from you in return."

He didn't have to say what the forfeit was, Yvonne had guessed it almost immediately. She looked around. The car park was about half full, but most of the vehicles were clustered along the opposite wall. A big square concrete pillar blocked the view of the attendant's box, so he wouldn't be able to see what was going on.

Licking her lips in anticipation, Yvonne sat up in her seat and reached through the window. She released the buttons of the jeans with nervous fingers that grew more confident as the contents were revealed. He was wearing no underwear, and she could easily pull the thick, warm trunk of his cock out when she had undone all the buttons.

The man moved closer to the car, and his erection pushed into the cabin. For a moment, Yvonne let it be, and it hovered before her, pointing upwards a little and demanding attention. She moved around on the seat, to face it straight on, and ran her tongue around the tip. The cock's owner shivered with pleasure as she took the big glans between her lips and played them back and forth over it. Her hand wrapped around the base, and she started taking more of the shaft into her mouth each time she bobbed her head forward.

Yvonne was skilled with her mouth and tongue. She practised new tricks on Tony all the time, which, of course, he encouraged. She used a few of them on the nameless cock sticking into her car, and its owner sounded like he was enjoying them. As well as moving her head back and forth, she started twisting it around the shaft as she moved. She could only move through a small angle, but it meant that her tongue rubbed against different sensitive spots on the way in and out.

The weight of the man beside the car shifted, as he tried to push more of himself through the window to get Yvonne's attentions. She was sure she felt the car shift, he was pressing so hard against it. He might hold the secret of her next move, but she was going to make sure he remembered giving it up. Pausing for a moment, she slobbered around the head with her tongue, then flicked the tip at the sensitive point where the glans bowed in toward the slit.

He was close to coming, Yvonne could tell. She ducked her head down and took as much of his length into her mouth as she could manage, then pulled back slowly, raking her tongue over

the underside of the hard on. Another couple of times doing this
and she felt the distinctive pulsing against her lips. Holding jus
the head in her mouth, she caught the full flow as he came.

When she had swallowed everything he pumped out, she le
the erection pop out of her mouth. It was glistening with he
saliva, and a red ring of lipstick marked just how deep she hac
been able to take it. Stepping back, its owner pulled an envelope
from his back pocket and passed it through the window. He
was still hard, barely subsiding after his orgasm, and had trouble
fitting back into his jeans. Yvonne watched his struggle for a
while, amused, then tore open the envelope.

'Why not go for a picnic. The guys will bring stuff to eat. T.'

Yvonne turned see if the stranger was still there, but he hac
disappeared. Yvonne fastened her seatbelt and started the ca
once the shivers of excitement had subsided a little. The
attendant waved at her as she exited, and she distractedl
returned the gesture as she pulled up the ramp to the street.

She knew exactly where she was going next. There was a
small picnic area a few miles out of town that she and Tony
would occasionally head to. In reality, it was just a single table
the heavy wooden type with integral bench seats, and was hardly
tended at all. Surrounded on three sides by trees, down a
neglected path and with no view to speak of, it wasn't popular
or well known. In all the times they had visited it, no-one else
had come along to interrupt them, whether they were eating or
making love.

Trying not to think of what might happen when she got
there- she needed to concentrate on her driving- Yvonne
navigated toward the picnic spot from memory. She stayed wel
within the speed limit, and was doubly attentive at traffic lights

and crossings. It wouldn't do to rush and miss out on the rest of the hunt because she crashed. So it took her longer than normal to reach the picnic spot.

There were no other cars in the concrete paved lot that was the nearest parking space to the picnic spot. The skeleton of the building that had previously occupied the space could be seen in the lines of brick in the concrete where walls had once been. Not for the first time, Yvonne wondered what purpose the building had served. But only for a while, she had a rendezvous to keep in the woodland beyond the lot.

One path, the widest, led away down to the river and some ponds which were popular with ducks and anglers. The other, narrower and partially overgrown, headed uphill. Wishing that she had changed shoes, Yvonne headed up this path. There was a short steep section, where someone had fashioned steps by planting thick boards into the earth to raise the levels of the path. Every time she took a step up one of, the loose front of her dress flapped open and she flashed the trees.

At the top of the steps, the path turned sharply left and Yvonne was in a green tunnel formed by the trees on either side, their branches reaching across to touch above her. It wasn't the exertion of the climb that had her heart beating when she spotted the two men standing by the picnic table.

One of them was Jason, still wearing the cycle courier outfit from the office. With the congestion in town, on top of her slow going, it wasn't surprising that he had reached the site by bike before she had. The other man was dressed similarly, and there were two bikes propped against trees on the edge of the clearing. Yvonne recognised him from pictures she had seen on The Gang. "Hello again, Jason. And.... Kevin, is it?"

"It is."

"You have the next clue?"

"We do." said Jason. "But we also have a challenge you have to complete before you can get it."

"Of course you do. What's the challenge?"

"Why, we are, of course?" said Kevin. He took a step toward Yvonne and offered her a hand. "Why don't you take a seat before we get started?"

Yvonne studied the table and its attached benches. The wood had darkened and weathered, and they were coated in leaves and dirt. "Not in my good dress. Look at it."

"There is an answer to that." Jason offered. He reached out to the front of her dress, hands hovering over the top button as he waited for permission.

Yvonne didn't even think about it, nodding enthusiastically. Jason started releasing the remaining closed buttons of her dress. When they were all undone, Kevin stepped round behind her and took the dress, lifting it off her shoulders, then gently folded it over his arm.

Now wearing just her bra and shoes, Yvonne clasped her hands behind her back and stood up straight for Jason's inspection. He liked what he saw. She looked down and saw the bulge in his trousers that proved it. "I think you could sit on the table now without spoiling your dress." he said.

Yvonne nodded eagerly. She took two steps backwards and sat on the end of the table, shuffling backwards and opening her legs. Jason stood in front of her and reached out to squeeze her breasts through her bra. "We'll leave this on for now. Got to be one last thing to remove at the finale."

"There's more?" Yvonne said with a squeak. Of course there was more. On a normal day, being naked in a wood with two strange men would have been the finale, but this wasn't any normal day. She was going to be fucked by two new cocks, and she'd already sucked another, but there'd be more to come after that. She looked around, and Kevin was carefully draping her dress over the handlebars of his bike. As he headed back, she pointed at the front of Jason's shorts and moved her finger up and down.

Jason was supposed to be taking charge, but he did exactly as he was told, unzipping his shorts as he stepped up to Yvonne. She pushed his hand aside and reached in to wrap fingers around his erection and pull it out. She looked down at it and smiled, then reclined on the grubby surface of the table.

She felt hands hooking under her knees and moving them apart and lifting them. Her pussy lips, hot and slick from the excitement that had been building since the first time she saw Jason, split and opened for him as he pressed the head of his cock to them. She exhaled slowly and loudly as he filled her in a long, slow thrust.

Hooking her legs around Jason's waist, Yvonne held him in place, savouring the size and length of him in her. The clearing rustled around them as the wind blew through the branches, and there was the sound of traffic far, far away, but the three people on and around the bench made no sound. As the silence drew out, Yvonne twisted her head to the side, to get a look at Kevin.

He was standing close to the table, watching the action, with an obvious hard on pushing out the front of his shorts. Yvonne nodded toward the bulge and raised her eyebrows. He quickly reached down and released it, revealing another fine cock, her third one so far today. She parted her lips, wetting them with the tip of her tongue, the invitation obvious.

Kevin climbed onto the bench, then placed his right knee on the table and leaned over Yvonne so that his erection pointed at her mouth. She grasped the base and pulled him toward her, slobbering her way down his shaft as Jason started pumping in and out of her. She tried to pass some of the pleasure coming from the cock in her pussy on to the one in her mouth. The noises Kevin was making, and the trembling that she could feel through the wood of the table, told her she was doing a good job of it.

Yvonne had had two men before. She and Tony had an out of office relationship with Beth and her husband, Gary, that was often carnal. She had taken both Tony and Gary at once, and watched Beth get the same treatment. She had 69'd Beth whilst their husbands did the same, and they had daisy-chained in all the combinations they could think of. Yvonne had a fair amount of experience, but this- being taken by two strangers out in the open- was a new experience. And she knew there would be more waiting for her wherever she ended up next.

Much more of Jason's hard and rhythmic pumping, and Yvonne would come. But this was all about tasting as many men as possible, taking as many as she could. She eased Kevin's cock from her mouth and said, simply, "Swap."

With the ease that could only come from having done this sort of thing before, Kevin and Jason changed places. Kevin took Yvonne's legs and rested them against his shoulders, so they were pointing straight up and he was entering her at a whole new angle compared to Jason. She liked it, certain he was going deeper. Jason's cock, meanwhile, waggled temptingly before her, glistening with her juices. She dragged it into her mouth, greedily slurping the taste of herself from him.

Yvonne loved tasting herself on a man. Possibly the only thing she enjoyed more was licking another woman's juices off her husband's cock. Her own lubrication was tangy and sharp, a reminder of the emotions and sensations that conjured it up.

They had all been close to the edge before the change around, and it didn't take long for the climaxes to start rolling. Jason came first, goaded on by Yvonne's talented tongue. He sighed and shivered above her as he pumped into her mouth. This load was saltier than the one she had taken in the car park, Yvonne thought. Much more of this and she would develop an expert's palate for semen. Her head at an angle, she couldn't keep all of it in her mouth, and some dribbled out of her lips to add another interesting stain to the wood of the table.

Jason's orgasm left Yvonne very close to her own. She barely had time to swallow what she could of his semen before a particularly hard and deep thrust from Kevin pushed her over the edge. She vocalised her joy around Jason's hard on, still in her mouth, and his shivers suggested he enjoyed the vibration of her moans. Kevin thrust fast and hard again, then again, then clasped her legs tight to his chest as he came, pumping deep inside her.

Kevin pulled out of Yvonne, and she felt sticky liquid drip out of her and between her butt cheeks. It was a wonderfully dirty feeling. He lowered her feet to the ground and, with Jason's aid, helped her stand up. More of his juices dripped down the insides of her legs. Kevin certainly delivered a big load, she thought.

"Let's clean some of that up before you put your good dres
back on." Jason offered, producing wipes from somewhere and
kneeling before her. The way he gently cleaned the sensitive skin
from her knees all the way up to the top of her thighs made
Yvonne shiver with anticipation of the next round.

She hadn't noticed Kevin wandering away, but when Jason
was done cleaning her up, he was there with her dress, ready to
drape it over her shoulders. He helped her into it, then Jason
fastened just one of the buttons. Now, when she walked, she
would not just risk flashing her pussy, but revealing her bra clad
breasts to anyone who looked.

"You have the next clue?" Yvonne asked.

Kevin handed her an envelope, which she ripped open
eagerly.

'The presentation should be ready by the time you get back
T.'

So, after being led away from the office, now she had to go
back again. Yvonne had sensed that Beth might be in on the
plan, and understood why she had handed over the office keys.
"How many are waiting for us there?" she asked.

"Oh, that would spoil the surprise." Jason said.

"I don't know if I can concentrate enough on driving to get
there in one piece."

"We thought of that. Luckily, I'm insured to drive any car."
Jason said. "You and Kevin can sit in the back while I chauffeur
you."

Yvonne looked sideways at Kevin, who gave her a knowing
smile. "Well, I guess my carriage awaits." she said.

They locked up Kevin and Jason's bikes by the car park, to be
recovered later, and Yvonne clambered into the back of her car,

to sit behind the driver's seat. She had never ridden in the back before, it was where the kids normally sat. Kevin was taller than her, and had a bit more trouble getting in. "Belt up." he said as he pulled his seat belt across his chest. Surely that would restrict their movements, Yvonne thought, but she pulled her own belt across and clicked it into place.

As the Mini pulled out of the car park, Kevin reached across and released the one fastened button on Yvonne's dress, pushing the flaps to either side to expose her body. Almost anyone who looked into the car would see her, but she didn't care.

The journey was smooth and controlled. Jason was obviously a professional driver, and Yvonne hardly noticed their motion through traffic. Particularly not when Kevin's hand slid under her seat belt and between her thighs. She spread her legs and he slid two fingers into her, entering easily on the juice he had left there.

Reaching across and curling around, Kevin's fingers couldn't get very far into Yvonne. But they rubbed against her clit and pressed and rotated on her mons, and that more than made up for it. They drove over a section of road where the tarmac had been ripped up before resurfacing, and the rough surface sent a vibration up through the seat and down through Kevin's fingers, making Yvonne moan and grasp the belt where it crossed her chest.

They came to a halt, and the engine stopped. Yvonne opened one eye and looked around. She was vaguely aware of where they were. Around the back of the block, there were four parking slots. They were usually reserved for Beth, Gary and the occasional workman, but Jason had pulled into one of them. On their left was Beth's BMW and to the right, Tony's VW Golf.

Kevin drew his fingers from Yvonne and she grabbed them to pull them to her lips and suck them. This time, as well as her own excitement, she got to taste Kevin's come.

Jason helped Yvonne from the car, and she gave him the keys Beth had handed her. "I think you'll need these to let us in." She didn't bother closing or buttoning her dress, which flapped behind her like a cape as they headed for the back door.

In the foyer, the door of the elevator was being held open by its occupants. Yvonne recognised Gary- the first man so far today who she had already had sex with- and the jeans the other guy wore were familiar. Kevin and Jason stopped her before she got to the elevator, and, once again, Kevin lifted the dress from her shoulders. "Gary and Brian will see you up to the meeting room." he said. "Jason and I will join you and everyone else shortly."

Yvonne stepped into the elevator and stood between the two attractive, and obviously excited men. She wore only her bra and boots, and, even before the doors had closed, Brian reached out and unclasped her bra.

She was proud of her breasts. Large, but not too big, and firm, they drooped ever so slightly when released from her bra. There was a delicious up tilt to them, her nipples pointed at a spot up the wall from her rather than at the ground. Gary and Brian appreciated them, too, each reaching out a hand to cup and squeeze one. They both dropped their heads to a nipple and sucked it, and as much as possible of the breast, into their mouths.

A hand, Yvonne didn't know whose, traced light touches down her stomach, across her mons and into her pussy. As they probed inside her, she couldn't help but rise up onto tiptoes, relying on the strong bodies pressed against her to stay balanced.

Another hand traced its way down her spine, stroked one buttock, then the other, then parted them.

Not even the support of the men either side of her could keep Yvonne upright now. She reached out, and found the wall by the button panel with one hand to help hold herself up. A finger pressed against the wrinkled opening of her arsehole, then squeezed in, and she moaned.

The elevator rocked as it came to a halt, and there was a ping. The doors opened on the top floor. Yvonne looked out, to see her husband looking back, a huge grin on his face. He wasn't at all perturbed to see his wife being fingered front and back by two other men, one of them a complete stranger. But then, the wife of one of the men playing with Yvonne was on her knees before Tony, giving him one of her enthusiastic blow jobs. Jason and Kevin hadn't made it up the stairs yet, but there were another two men standing behind Tony and Beth, both of them naked and well hung.

"The birthday girl's here." Tony said. "The party can really begin now. Bring her in and lay her on the table would you, guys."

Gary and Brian took their fingers out of Yvonne and lifted her between them, making her squeal at the sudden movement. They carried her out of the elevator and into Meeting Room Two. Laid out on one end of the table was a cake, lots of snack food and bottles of beer and wine. In the centre of the table were the lacy panties she had removed so long ago. Gary and Brian sat her on the end of the table nearest the window- the birthday girl ready to receive the rest of her gifts.

As Beth helped Gary and Brian undress, Tony stood before Yvonne, looking her over with lust and love. "How's your birthday?"

She grabbed him and pulled him to her to kiss him passionately, wrapping her legs around his waist and holding him tight. "Best. Birthday. Ever." she said, punctuating each word with a kiss.

"And there's more." Tony announced, when Yvonne had stopped kissing him. He waved at the two men who had been standing behind him when the elevator doors opened. "This is Steve and Curt. They came along in case the five of us weren't enough." he said. "As you can see, they really hope you'll let them join in."

Seven men, Yvonne thought, dizzy at the idea. Well, she had given three men blow jobs so far today, taken two in her pussy, and been fingered by three. Was that everything? She couldn't remember. Seven men, and no doubt Beth would want to join in somehow. Could she take them all?

There was only one way to find out. She'd give it a try. It was her birthday, after all, and she could take the weekend to recover.

"I need someone in my arse." Yvonne announced. She pointed. "Curt?" He nodded. "Would you like to bugger me?"

Curt stepped forward, and Tony took a step back. At a nod from him, Yvonne turned around and lay on her front on the table, legs hanging over the edge. Strong hands kneaded her buttocks, parting them and then squeezing them together. Then a thumb pressed at the muscle of her sphincter, squeezing into her, getting her ready. She reached out to her sides and clasped the edges of the table as the thumb withdrew and she felt the rounded glans of Curt's penis pressing at the entrance.

Looking up, Yvonne could see everyone else had gathered at the other end of the table. Kevin and Jason had arrived, and quickly stripped off and now they were all naked and watching her and Curt. They each had a glass of wine or bottle of beer and they saluted her with them as Curt pushed in.

"Best birthday ever." Yvonne repeated ecstatically as the head of Curt's cock squeezed past the ring of muscle and entered her.

Don't miss out!

Visit the website below and you can sign up to receive emails whenever Mary Tales publishes a new book. There's no charge and no obligation.

https://books2read.com/r/B-A-XESE-QLVR

BOOKS 2 READ

Connecting independent readers to independent writers.

Also by Mary Tales

Jiggles
Jiggles and the Test Pilot
Jiggles and the Archaeologists
Jiggles and the Flying Boats

Love By The Book
Love By The Book
Love The Weekend

Mary Tales Collections
Mary Tales Omnibus
Contact Adventures
Contact Adventures 2 - First Timers
Cassie Gets it On
The Adventures of Jiggles

Meet The Gang

Meet The Gang